The Emperor's New Clothes

Retold by Karen Wallace

Illustrated by François Hall

FRANKLIN WATTS
LONDON•SYDNEY

The Emperor's New Clothes

First published in 2005 by
Franklin Watts
96 Leonard Street
London
EC2A 4XD

Franklin Watts Australia
45–51 Huntley Street
Alexandria
NSW 2015

A CIP catalogue record for this book is available
from the British Library.

ISBN 0 7496 6151 8 (hbk)
ISBN 0 7496 6163 1 (pbk)

Series Editor: Jackie Hamley
Series Advisor: Dr Barrie Wade
Series Designer: Peter Scoulding

Printed in Hong Kong / China

Once there lived an
Emperor who loved
expensive clothes.

5

Two men decided to cheat him. "We can make you some special cloth.

It's so special that stupid people cannot see it," they said.

The Emperor gave the cheats lots of money and gold thread to make the special cloth.

Soon, the Emperor came to
visit the cheats' workshop.
The cheats pretended to
show the Emperor his cloth.

But, of course, he could see
nothing! He thought people
would call him stupid, so he
said: "What beautiful cloth!"

His courtiers couldn't see the cloth either. But no one wanted to look stupid.

So they all said: "Emperor, this cloth is the most beautiful cloth ever made!"

"Make me some new clothes by tomorrow," said the Emperor. "I will wear them for the procession!"

The cheats pretended to
cut the cloth with scissors.

Then they pretended to
sew the pieces together.

The Emperor stood
in front of a mirror.
"Here are your trousers
and coat," said the cheats.
"They are so light, you
will not feel them."

19

The cheats pretended to
help the Emperor dress.

The Emperor pretended he could see his new clothes.

Everyone stared as the Emperor walked at the front of the procession.

But they all pretended
they could see his
new clothes.

Suddenly, a little boy shouted: "The Emperor has no clothes on!"

Everyone started to laugh.
"Look at the Emperor!
He isn't wearing
any clothes!"

The Emperor knew it
was true, but what
could he do?

He had to finish the
procession with no
clothes on!

And the cheats quickly left town with their bags full of money and gold thread!

Leapfrog has been specially designed to fit the requirements of the National Literacy Strategy. It offers real books for beginning readers by top authors and illustrators.

There are 31 Leapfrog stories to choose from:

The Bossy Cockerel
Written by Margaret Nash, illustrated by Elisabeth Moseng

Bill's Baggy Trousers
Written by Susan Gates, illustrated by Anni Axworthy

Mr Spotty's Potty
Written by Hilary Robinson, illustrated by Peter Utton

Little Joe's Big Race
Written by Andy Blackford, illustrated by Tim Archbold

The Little Star
Written by Deborah Nash, illustrated by Richard Morgan

The Cheeky Monkey
Written by Anne Cassidy, illustrated by Lisa Smith

Selfish Sophie
Written by Damian Kelleher, illustrated by Georgie Birkett

Recycled!
Written by Jillian Powell, illustrated by Amanda Wood

Felix on the Move
Written by Maeve Friel, illustrated by Beccy Blake

Pippa and Poppa
Written by Anne Cassidy, illustrated by Philip Norman

Jack's Party
Written by Ann Bryant, illustrated by Claire Henley

The Best Snowman
Written by Margaret Nash, illustrated by Jörg Saupe

Eight Enormous Elephants
Written by Penny Dolan, illustrated by Leo Broadley

Mary and the Fairy
Written by Penny Dolan, illustrated by Deborah Allwright

The Crying Princess
Written by Anne Cassidy, illustrated by Colin Paine

Jasper and Jess
Written by Anne Cassidy, illustrated by François Hall

The Lazy Scarecrow
Written by Jillian Powell, illustrated by Jayne Coughlin

The Naughty Puppy
Written by Jillian Powell, illustrated by Summer Durantz

Freddie's Fears
Written by Hilary Robinson, illustrated by Ross Collins

Cinderella
Written by Barrie Wade, illustrated by Julie Monks

The Three Little Pigs
Written by Maggie Moore, illustrated by Rob Hefferan

Jack and the Beanstalk
Written by Maggie Moore, illustrated by Steve Cox

The Three Billy Goats Gruff
Written by Barrie Wade, illustrated by Nicola Evans

Goldilocks and the Three Bears
Written by Barrie Wade, illustrated by Kristina Stephenson

Little Red Riding Hood
Written by Maggie Moore, illustrated by Paula Knight

Rapunzel
Written by Hilary Robinson, illustrated by Martin Impey

Snow White
Written by Anne Cassidy, illustrated by Melanie Sharp

The Emperor's New Clothes
Written by Karen Wallace, illustrated by François Hall

The Pied Piper of Hamelin
Written by Anne Adeney, illustrated by Jan Lewis

Hansel and Gretel
Written by Penny Dolan, illustrated by Graham Philpot

The Sleeping Beauty
Written by Margaret Nash, illustrated by Barbara Vagnozzi